STEVENSON-BRIT
ADULT LEARN
CENTRE

The Kit Kat
Charmaine Marrochia

Copyright © 2004 Charmaine Marrochia
Illustrations, Heather Dickinson
Cover Design, Mike Carter
Editor, Steph Prior

First published and distributed by New Leaf Readers in 2006

Printed by RAP Spiderweb, Oldham
ISBN 1-905688-06-7 and 978-1-905688-06-7

British Library cataloguing in publication data: A catalogue record for this book is available from the British Library

New Leaf Publishing is a member of The Federation of Worker Writers & Community Publishers.

We are extremely grateful for financial support from
The UnLtd Millennium Awards Scheme

It was the week before Christmas.
I had been shopping with my friend.

As we were going to the bus stop we said we would call in for a coffee in a nearby café.

When we called in to the café
it was so busy.
There was nowhere to sit.

There was an old man on his own.
We went
to sit with him.

I went to the counter
to get two cups of coffee
and a Kit Kat.

I took them to the table
and went back to the counter
to get some sugar.

When I sat down to drink my coffee,
the old man picked up the Kit Kat.
He broke a piece off.

I then broke a piece off
and so did my friend.

The old man then took the last piece.

Me and my friend
looked at each other.
We thought,
"What a rude old man!"

Then the old man got up.
He bought a sticky bun
and sat back down
at the table.

Just before we left
the café,
my friend said,
"I will get him back.
Watch this!"

She picked up his bun
and took a large bit [bite] out of it.
"That's for eating our Kit Kat!"
she said.

When I got on the bus with my friend
I put my hand in my pocket
to get my purse out
to pay the fare.

Guess what I found......?
My Kit Kat!

About the Author

I want to dedicate this book
to my daughter, Cheri,
because of all the encouragement
she has given me.
The Kit Kat is a true story
that happened to me.

Thanks also to Mary,
my English teacher.
Coming to her classes,
meeting new people
and sharing things together
has given me more confidence.
I have read a few books like this
and I hope you will enjoy reading mine.

Everyone in my English class
entered a writing competition.
We all got a letter back.
I couldn't believe it when I looked at mine
and it said I'd won!

When the letter came from New Leaf
to say they wanted to publish my story
I was a bit nervous but so proud
as it was a big achievement.
I showed the letter to my daughter, Cheri.
She said, "Go on, Mum.
Get in touch with them!"

Charmaine Marrochia

What is New Leaf?

New Leaf is a brand new and unique community publishing project set up to publish and promote writing by ordinary people who would normally never expect to see their own words in print. We aim to develop adults' reading and writing skills using creative reading and writing activities and by publishing writings by and for adults who are working to improve their reading and writing skills.

Although we are new, we are not wet behind the ears! The project has been set up by two dedicated and experienced community publishers who have both worked in this field for many years for different organisations which have now sadly disappeared. We were determined that tried and tested methods and principles which have proved so successful many times over must not be lost. We see ourselves as the true descendants of a proud tradition which has been established over the last thirty years and which we will carry forward to a brighter future!

Booklist available

New Leaf Readers
5, Cranleigh Close
Walton
Warrington
WA4 6SD
Tel: 07984 241 863
E-mail: info@newleafpublishing.org.uk
www.newleafpublishing.org.uk